Padma Shri Pran

Maurice Horn, the editor of World Encyclopedia of Comics, has described cartoonist PRAN as Walt Disney of India.

Entertaining generation after generation, his comics have been constant companion of all the growing youngsters providing fun and amusement through his famous characters like CHACHA CHAUDHARY, SABU, SHRIMATIJI, PINKI, BILLOO, RAMAN etc. More than 600 of his titles are selling well in the market, and numerous comic strips are regularly appearing in various newspapers. His CHACHA CHAUDHARY comics had already been adapted for a TV Serial, and ran continuously for 600 episodes on a premier channel.

Travelling widely over the globe, he delivers lectures at various International Conferences. He has also been honoured with 'People of The Year Award' by Limca Book of Records for popularizing comics. His comic book 'United We Stand' was released in 1983 by the then Prime Minister Mrs. Indira Gandhi, and is still very popular among children.

Publisher

PINKI'S ICE CREAM

LET'S NOT ACCEPT DEFEAT SO EASILY . WE WON'T LET PINKI WALK AWAY WITH THE TROPHY.

WE'LL EARN MAXIMUM WITHOUT THE STALL.
PINKI SUPER ICE CREAM
I UNDERSTAND. WE'LL HAVE TO ACTIVATE OUR SUPER PLAN.

PINKI SUPER ICE CREAM
BHIKHU'S PIZZA
CHAMPU'S CHOWMEI
THIS TIME OUR PLAN WILL BE SUCCESSFUL. HA-HA-HA...!
FUNFAIR ORGANIZED BY KIDS.

BITTI. YOU'RE NOT PUTTING UP A STALL ?

NO, I THOUGHT OF HELPING YOU RATHER. I'LL SELL THE ICE CREAM IF A CUSTOMER COMES
OK BITTI.

PINKI THERE ARE 2 FREEZERS HERE WHICH ONE IS YOURS?
THIS ONE ON THE RIGHT. THE OTHER ONE BELONGS TO THE COMPANY WILL TAKE IT IN SOME TIME. I'LL JUST BE BACK BITTI.

PINKI SAID THAT THE ONE ON THE RIGHT IS HERS. BUT SHE WAS STANDING OPPOSITE TO ME. SO THE ONE ON THE RIGHT MEANS HER RIGHT OR MY RIGHT?

MUST BE THIS ONE. IT'S OPENED. I'LL TAKE ALL THE ICE CREAM FROM IT AND KEEP IT IN MY BAG. THEN ACCORDING TO THE PLAN I'LL SELL IT ON HALF PRICE ALONG WITH NATTU.

BANG!!!

DUE TO THE TRUCK BREAKING DOWN, I HAD TO LEAVE THIS FREEZER HERE. I'LL LOCK IT AND HAVE SOME SNACKS.

WHERE'S BITTI ? THANK GOD I RETURNED. NOW I'LL SELL ICE CREAM TO ALL THE CUSTOMERS.

FUN FAIR HAS STARTED. PEOPLE ARE COMING. THIS TIME THERE'S A BIGGER CROWD. THERE SHOULD BE A WONDERFUL SALE.

GIVE ME A VANILLA ICE CREAM.
A STRAWBERRY.
A BUTTER SCOTCH.

INSIDE THE FREEZER
OH ! SOMEONE HAS LOCKED THE FREEZER. I THINK I'VE ENTERED THE WRONG FREEZER. IT'S SO FREEZING HERE.
IT'S STRANGE. BITTI HASN'T REACHED AS YET. ACCORDING TO THE PLAN WE HAD TO STEAL PINKI'S ICE CREAM AND SELL IT AT HALF PRICE OUTSIDE THE SCHOOL.

WOW! AMAZING SALE AND WONDERFUL PROFIT. IT SEEMS I'LL BE THE WINNER THIS YEAR ALSO.

THE STALL WHICH HAD THE MAXIMUM SALE IS PINKI'S SUPER ICE CREAM STALL. PINKI COME AND TAKE YOUR TROPHY.

THANK YOU.

PINKI HAS WON THE TROPHY. GOD KNOWS WHERE'S BITTI

PINKI HAVE YOU SEEN BITTI?
YES, SHE DID MEET ME. BUT I DON'T KNOW WHERE SHE WENT AFTER THAT.

INSIDE THE FREEZER.
IT'S SO COLD HERE. IT SEEMS I'LL ALSO FREEZE HERE.

BITTI WHERE ARE YOU ?
NATTU IS AN ABSOLUTE FOOL. WHY IS HE NOT OPENING THE FREEZER ?
I SOLD THE ENTIRE ICE CREAM. I WANT ONE FOR MYSELF.

UNCLE ! WHERE ARE YOU TAKING THIS FREEZER ?
TO THE COMPANY.
ICE CREAM

WHY NOT ? YOU GAVE A PROFIT TO THE COMPANY. YOU'LL DEFINITELY GET 1 ICE CREAM. I'LL OPEN THE FREEZER.

BITTI ? YOU ??? HERE ???

PRAN'S
CHACHA CHAUDHARY
AND
KUMBH MELA
Kumbh Special
PRAYAGRAJ 2019
Makar Sankranti 25 January 2019
Pus full moon 21 January 2019
Maun Amavasya 04 Feb 2019
Vasant Panchami 10 February 2019
Maghi Purnima, 19 February 2019
Maha Shivratri 04 March 2019

CHACHA CHAUDHARY
AND
KUMBH MELA

PADAMSHRI PRAN

Prayagraj Kumbh 2019, is considered as the world's largest grand, religious and spiritual fair.

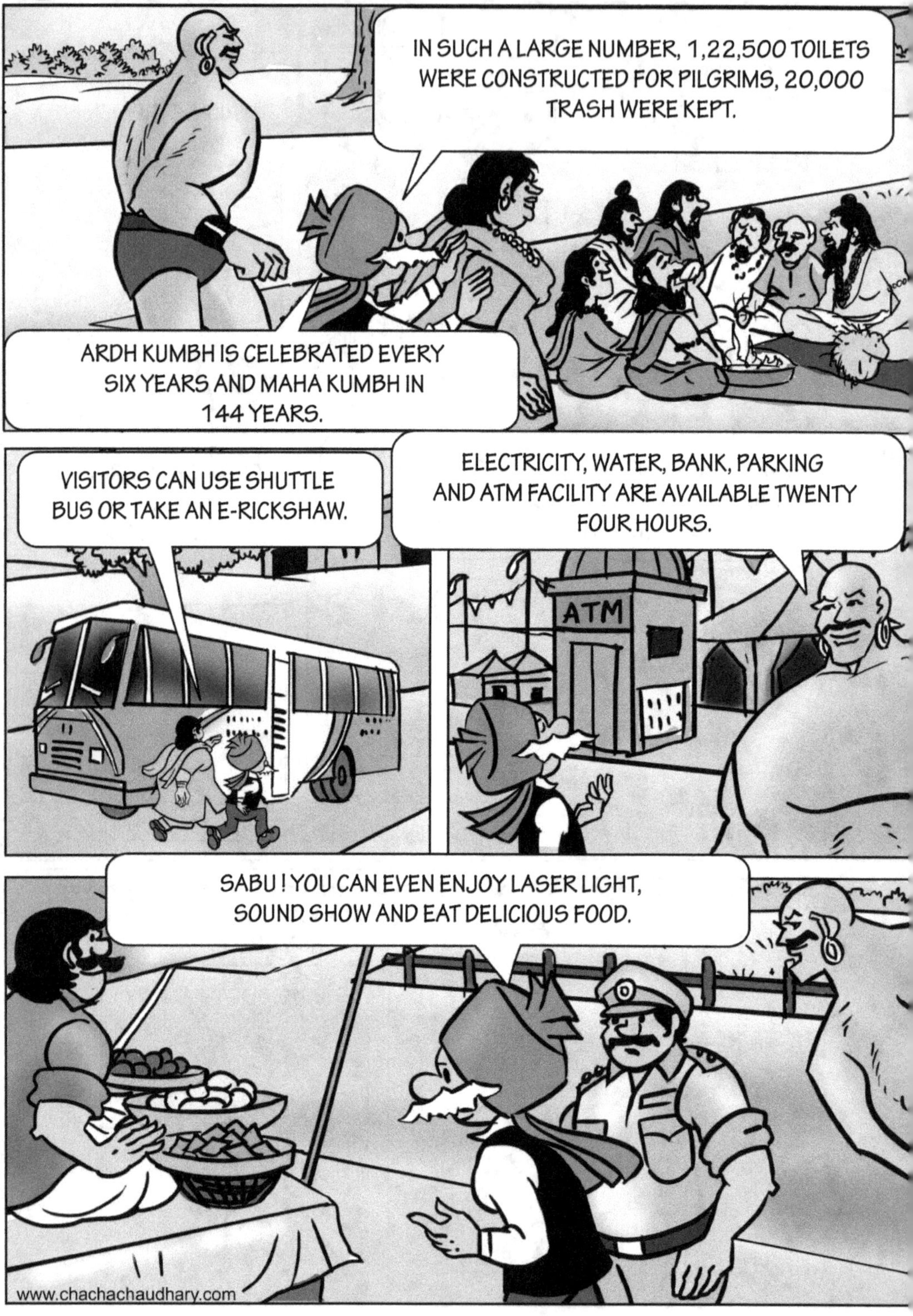

IN SUCH A LARGE NUMBER, 1,22,500 TOILETS WERE CONSTRUCTED FOR PILGRIMS, 20,000 TRASH WERE KEPT.
ARDH KUMBH IS CELEBRATED EVERY SIX YEARS AND MAHA KUMBH IN 144 YEARS.
VISITORS CAN USE SHUTTLE BUS OR TAKE AN E-RICKSHAW.
ELECTRICITY, WATER, BANK, PARKING AND ATM FACILITY ARE AVAILABLE TWENTY FOUR HOURS.
ATM
SABU ! YOU CAN EVEN ENJOY LASER LIGHT, SOUND SHOW AND EAT DELICIOUS FOOD.

HOSPITAL
ALL THE WALLS OF GOVERNMENT BUILDINGS AND FLYOVERS HAVE BEEN PAINTED WITH PAINTINGS UNDER 'PAINT MY CITY' PROGRAMM.
DIGITAL SCREEN.
THIS IS OUR CONTROL ROOM.
ZOOM ON THAT PERSON.

For the Kumbh, Uttar Pradesh government has allocated 4200 crore rupees, which is 3 times more than the Kumbh 2013. More than 6 lakh people are estimated to be employed

SABU ! CATCH HIM.

HUBBA ! HUBBA !!
YOU CAN'T
DESTROY
KUMBH MELA.

NO ONE CAN
STOP GORA !
HA ! HA !!

SABU ! FORMULA
NO. 265.

Kumbh in numerals- 2000 years old tradition, 33 crore Gods & Goddess, 55 days, 14 akhada, 12 million pilgrims, 3200 hectare fair area, 36 crores meals, 192 countries, more than 30,000 medical staff, 45,000 police personnel

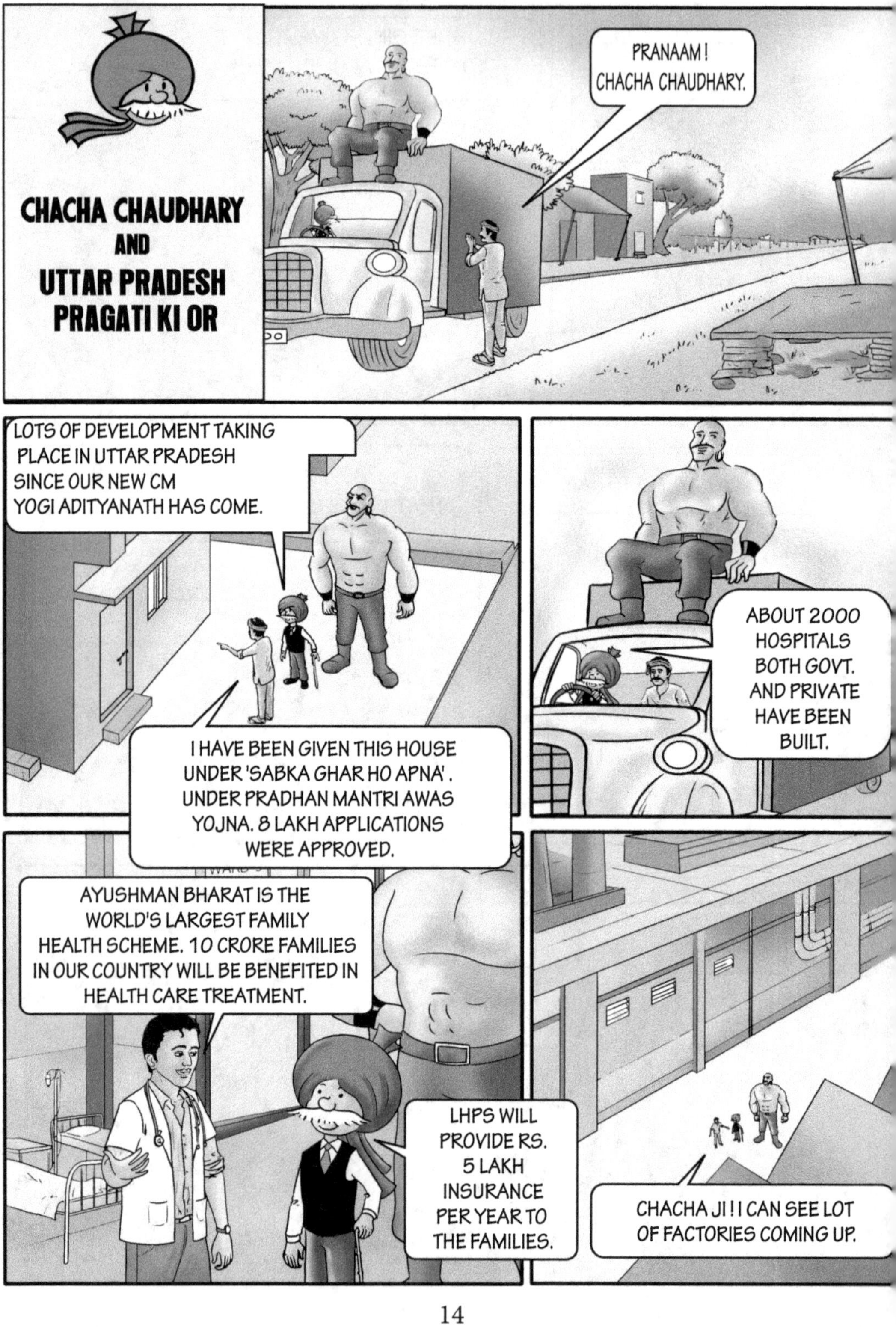

CHACHA CHAUDHARY
AND
UTTAR PRADESH PRAGATI KI OR

FOR EVERY DEVELOPMENT YOU NEED INVESTMENT.
I HAVE BEEN ABLE TO GET LAND FOR MY INDUSTRY ON CHEAP AND EASY LOANS FROM THE BANKS WITH 24 HR ELECTRICITY AND WATER SUPPLY.
OUR CHIEF MINISTER IS DOING GREAT WORK FOR DEVELOPMENT OF U.P. STATE.
MORE THAN 60,000 CRORE RUPEES WILL BE INVESTED IN VARIOUS SCHEMES TO BRING UP INDUSTRIES.
LET'S SEE WHAT IS BEING DONE IN EDUCATION FIELD IN UTTAR PRADESH.
WE ARE COMPUTERIZING THE DATA OF EACH STUDENT AND TEACHER. RS 500 CRORE HAVE BEEN ALLOCATED TO PROVIDE FACILITIES LIKE FURNITURE, ELECTRICITY AND WATER IN THE SCHOOLS.
ENROLLMENT OF MORE THAN 1,31,163 STUDENTS UNDER SCHOOL CHALO ABHIYAN SCHEME.
PRINCIPAL

For the first time, the whole fair is under surveillance of CCTV. The entire fair has 40 fire stations, 40 surveillance towers, 62 police posts, and 3 women police stations.

15

CHACHA JI, LET'S MEET BHIM SINGH. HE GROWS SUGAR CANE IN HIS FIELDS.
NAMASTE ! CHACHAJI.
NOW YOU MUST BE HAPPY THAT GOVT. WILL DAY ALL THE DUES TO SUGARCANE GROWERS.
YES ! THAT'S TRUE. WE WERE REALLY VERY UPSET BEFORE.
IN 2017-18 UP GOVT. HAS PAID RS 27,729.48 CRORE TO SUGARCANE FARMERS AND DURING THIS PERIOD. A RECORD PRODUCTION OF SUGAR HAS BEEN REGISTERD
CHIEF MINISTER YOGI ADITYANATH WANTED TO DOUBLE THE FARMERS INCOME BY 2022.
I CAN SEE A TOILET HERE. 1.71 CRORE TOILETS HAVE BEEN BUILT FOR 2.5 CRORE FAMILIES IN UP UNDER 'SWACHH BHARAT' ABHIYAN.

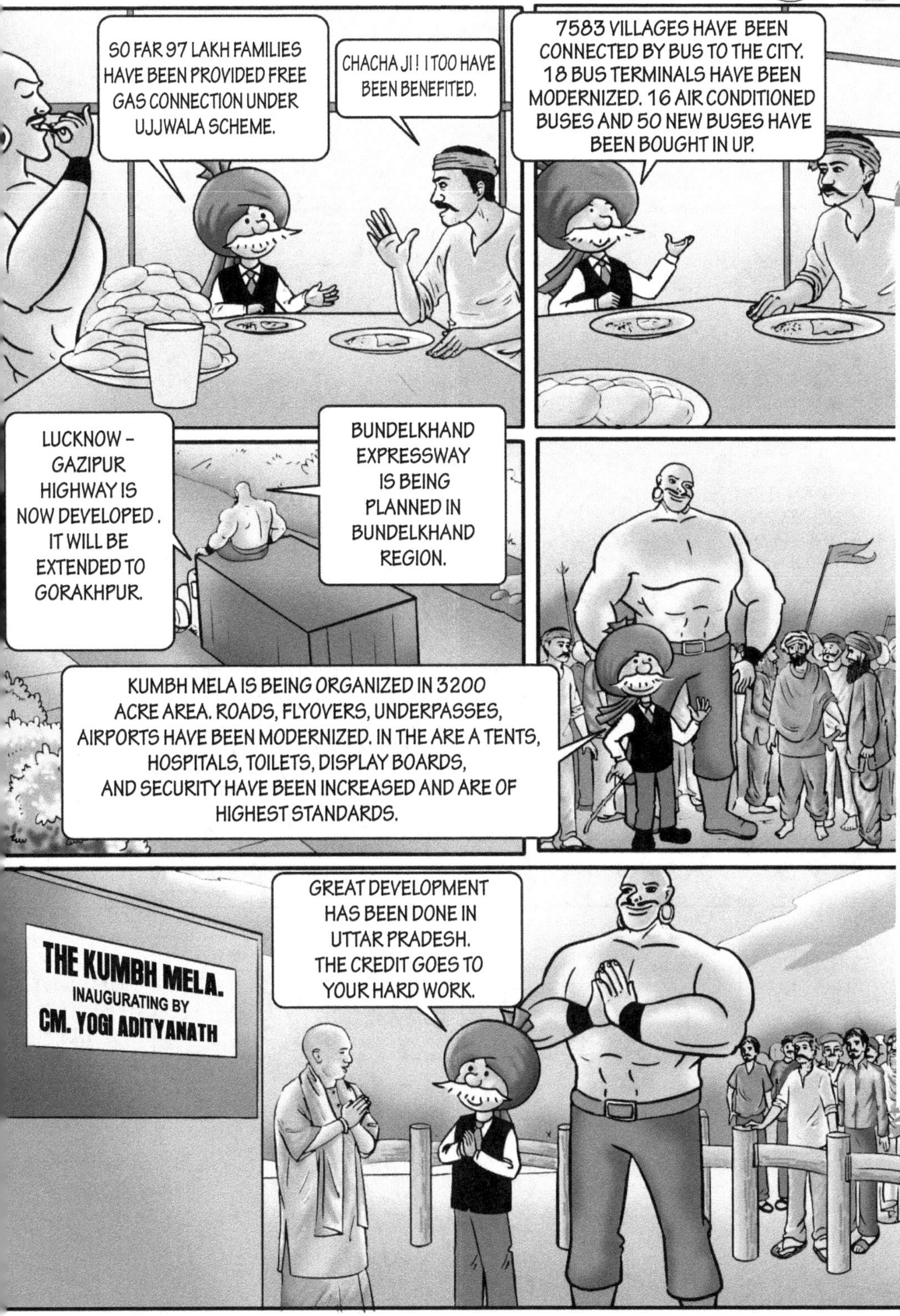

SO FAR 97 LAKH FAMILIES HAVE BEEN PROVIDED FREE GAS CONNECTION UNDER UJJWALA SCHEME.
CHACHA JI ! I TOO HAVE BEEN BENEFITED.
7583 VILLAGES HAVE BEEN CONNECTED BY BUS TO THE CITY. 18 BUS TERMINALS HAVE BEEN MODERNIZED. 16 AIR CONDITIONED BUSES AND 50 NEW BUSES HAVE BEEN BOUGHT IN UP.
LUCKNOW – GAZIPUR HIGHWAY IS NOW DEVELOPED . IT WILL BE EXTENDED TO GORAKHPUR.
BUNDELKHAND EXPRESSWAY IS BEING PLANNED IN BUNDELKHAND REGION.
KUMBH MELA IS BEING ORGANIZED IN 3200 ACRE AREA. ROADS, FLYOVERS, UNDERPASSES, AIRPORTS HAVE BEEN MODERNIZED. IN THE ARE A TENTS, HOSPITALS, TOILETS, DISPLAY BOARDS, AND SECURITY HAVE BEEN INCREASED AND ARE OF HIGHEST STANDARDS.
THE KUMBH MELA.
INAUGURATING BY
CM. YOGI ADITYANATH
GREAT DEVELOPMENT HAS BEEN DONE IN UTTAR PRADESH. THE CREDIT GOES TO YOUR HARD WORK.
Uttar Pradesh is the country's third largest system. in 2017-18, a total of 9.10 lakh houses were sanctioned under the Prime Minister's Housing Scheme.

PINKI
GRANDPA'S VALENTINE'S DAY
TODAY'S VALENTINE'S DAY. ALL THE HUSBANDS HAVE PURCHASED GIFTS FOR THEIR WIVES.
OH! SO TODAY'S VALENTINE'S DAY. BUT PINKI'S DADAJI HAS NEVER GIVEN ME A GIFT.
OH GOD! THERE'S NOT EVEN A SINGLE FLOWER TODAY.
LISTEN! THE PAPER SAYS THAT TODAY'S VALENTINE'S DAY. ALL THE HUSBANDS GIFT SOMETHING TO THEIR WIVES.
WHAT'S THIS TROUBLE NOW?
THEY ARE TALES AND NOT THE REALITY.
I DON'T KNOW ALL THAT. JUST GIFT ME A BIG FLOWER.
BUT I WANT IT BEFORE 12 TODAY. OTHERWISE YOU WON'T GET FOOD.

OH GOD! IT'S ALREADY 11. WHERE WILL I GET A FLOWER SO SOON?

IDEA!! I'LL ASK THE FLORIST FOR ONE FLOWER. HE WON'T CHARGE ME FOR ONE FLOWER. BOTH MY POCKET AND PINKI'S DADI WILL BE HAPPY!! HA-HA-HA!!

I WANT A FLOWER.
YOU'RE WELCOME. TELL ME WHICH FLOWER DO YOU REQUIRE?

CAN YOU GIVE ME A BIG FLOWER FOR FREE?
YOU WON'T GET EVEN A PETAL FREE OF COST.

GO AWAY FROM HERE.
HOW RUDE? THERE'S NO GOODNESS IN PEOPLE THESE DAYS.

लवली फ्लॉवर
WOW! ANOTHER FLOWER SHOP. THE BOY SITTING HERE IS YOUNG AND WILL UNDERSTAND MY FEELINGS. BUT THIS TIME I'LL PURCHASE A FLOWER.
I WANT A FLOWER.
TAKE IT! WHAT'S YOUR BUDGET?
HERE, TAKE RS 5 AND GIVE A BEAUTIFUL FLOWER.
THESE ARE IMPORTED FLOWERS. EACH ONE COSTS NOT LESS THAN RS. 500.
SO EXPENSIVE! IN OUR DAYS WE USED TO PURCHASE GOLD IN RS 500.
THEN GO AND PURCHASE IT FROM YOUR ERA. WHY ARE YOU WASTING TIME HERE?
STRANGE! TIMES HAVE CHANGED SO MUCH. I COULDN'T GET A FLOWER HERE ALSO. WHAT TO DO?

IF I DON'T GIVE A FLOWER TO PINKI'S DADI TILL 12, I'LL HAVE TO REMAIN HUNGRY.

THIS IS HARIYA'S GARDEN. HE'S A MISER BUT I'LL PLUCK ONE FLOWER. HE WON'T EVEN KNOW.

WOW ! SUCH BIG ROSES AND NOONE IS THERE TO STOP. TODAY PINKI'S DADI WILL ALSO AGREE THAT I CAN GIFT HER A WONDERFUL FLOWER.

HARIYA! YOU'RE HERE ?
YES, I'M HERE. YOU'LL SURELY GET A ROSE. BUT YOU'LL HAVE TO PLAY WITH BITTOO FOR SOME TIME. HE'S GETTING BORED.

OH ! I'VE PLAYED WITH SO MANY BITTOOS. WHERE'S YOURS? I'LL PLAY WITH IT JUST NOW.

THIS IS BITTOO.

BITTOO IS THE NAME OF A DOG?

DADAJI!
PINKI! I'M ALREADY VERY TROUBLED. DON'T IRRITATE ME FURTHER.

THAT'S WHAT I WANT TO KNOW. TELL ME THE CAUSE OF WORRY. I MAY BE ABLE TO SOLVE IT. DID YOU NOT GET THE NEWSPAPER TODAY?

YOUR DADI READ THAT TODAY IS VALENTINE'S DAY. SHE IS INSISTING THAT I GIFT HER A BIG ROSE.
THAT'S IT? THEN GIFT A BIG FLOWER TO HER.

I DON'T WANT TO SPEND MORE THAN RS. 5 AND TODAY ALL THE FLOWERS ARE VERY EXPENSIVE.

IN RS 5 YOU'LL GET THIS BIG FLOWER.
REALLY ! IF YOU DO THAT, I'LL FETCH YOU AN ICE CREAM.

YOU GO TO DADI. I'LL GET A BIG FLOWER FOR YOU TO GIFT HER.
I'LL REACH THERE SOON.

HAVE YOU BROUGHT A BIG FLOWER FOR ME ?
WAIT FOR 2 MINUTES. YOU'LL GET A BIG FLOWER.

OH ! A CAULI-FLOWER !!

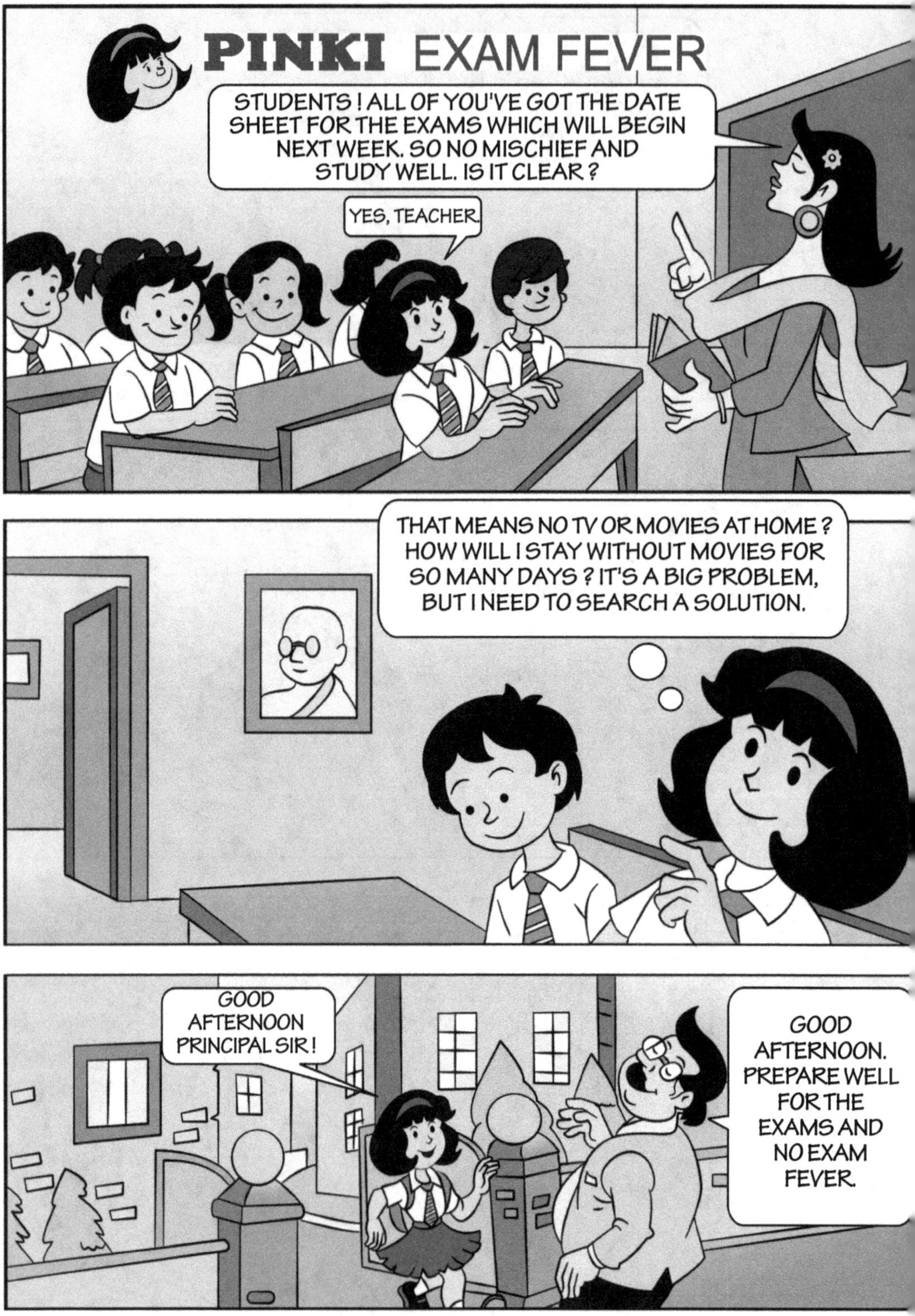

PINKI — EXAM FEVER

WHAT'S THAT SIR?
WHEN STUDENTS WORRY TOO MUCH ABOUT THE EXAMS, THEY GET A FEVER THAT'S CALLED EXAM FEVER. KIDS AREN'T ABLE TO STUDY DUE TO THIS.

IT SEEMS, I'VE FOUND A SOLUTION.

MADHU I'VE BROUGHT THE CD OF A LATEST MOVIE. WHY NOT WATCH IT?
HIDE IT KASHAB! IF PINKI SEES IT, SHE'LL INSIST ON WATCHING THE MOVIE. SHE HAS HER EXAMS. WE'LL WATCH IT AFTER SHE SLEEPS.

IT SEEMS PINKI'S BACK.
I'LL JUST OPEN THE DOOR.

PINKI! WHAT HAPPENED? WHY ARE SITTING HERE?
I FEEL FEVERISH! I'M FEELING VERY WEAK ALSO.

THIS IS A DIFFERENT FEVER. EXAM FEVER. THE THERMOMETER WILL SHOW THIS.

HERE TAKE IT PINKY! CHECK YOUR FEVER.
SURE! BUT I WANT WARM MILK FIRST. I'M FEELING VERY WEAK.

TAKE THE MILK PINKI. AFTER THAT CHECK YOUR FEVER WITH THE THERMOMETER. I'LL JUST FINISH MY WORK IN THE KITCHEN AND COME.

NOW THE TEMPERATURE OF THIS THERMOMETER WILL SOAR SO MUCH THAT MOM DAD WILL TELL ME TO REMAIN AWAY FROM MY BOOKS AND I'LL ENJOY THE MOVIES. HA-HA-HA…

PINKI! DID YOU DRINK MILK?
I DIDN'T FEEL LIKE. BUT I'VE TAKEN THE TEMPERATURE.

OH GOD ! IT SHOWS 106*.
KASHAB CALL THE DOCTOR QUICKLY. THE SITUATION IS SERIOUS.

HELLO ! DR RUNJHUNWALA AND DR JHUMJHUMWALA'S SECRETARY SANDWICH SPEAKING. HOW MAY I HELP YOU ?
PINKI'S SUFFERING FROM A STRANGE FEVER WHICH CAN'T BE CHECKED BY TOUCH, BUT ONLY BY A THERMOMETER. CAN YOU CURE HER ?
WHY NOT ? I'LL DO IT RIGHT NOW.

I CAN'T DECIDE WHOM SHALL I ASK TO SEE PINKI.

SANDWICH ! I GIVE HALF OF YOUR. I'LL GO .
YOUR OTHER HALF SALARY I GIVE. SO I'LL GO.

COME ! LET'S BOTH GO AND SEE THE PATIENT. WE'LL PROVE THAT WE ARE ABLE DOCTORS.
I FEEL THAT YOU BOTH SHOULD GO AND SEE THE PATIENT. PINKI'S FEELING COLD BUT IT'S NOT SHOWING IN THERMOMETER.

PINKI IS NOT ABLE TO STUDY DUE TO FEVER.
LET HER WATCH A MOVIE. SHE'LL BE BUSY.

WOW ! EXAM FEVER IS GREAT. IT WON'T GO SO EASILY. HA ! HA !!
DOCTOR ! YOU BOTH ! AND SO MANY BOOKS.
SANDWICH TOLD US IT'S A COMPLICATED CASE. WE NEED BOOKS FOR REFERENCE PURPOSE.

THE DOOR BELL IS RINGING.
DOCTOR MUST BE THERE.
JHUNJHUN WALA ! PINKI'S FEVER IS A COMBINATION BE A FEVER. EXAM FEVER AND MALARIA.
RUNJHUN WALA ! I DISAGREE WITH YOU. IT'S A MIX OF A FEVER, EXAM FEVER AND VIRAL.

I CAN'T BE WRONG. I HAVEN'T GROWN THIS BEARD LIKE THIS ONLY.
AND I HAVEN'T BECOME BALD WITH MY EXPERIENCE JUST LIKE THAT.

OH ! PLEASE DON'T FIGHT.
DING-DONG...

PAPA ! PINKI'S SUFFERING FROM A STRANGE FEVER WHICH CAN'T BE CHECKED BY TOUCH, BUT ONLY BY A THERMOMETER. CAN YOU CURE HER ?
WHY NOT ? I'LL DO IT RIGHT NOW.
PINKI MUST HAVE PUT THE THERMOMETER IN SOMETHING HOT. I'LL PUT ICE IN THAT.

PINKI CAN YOU CHECK THE TEMPERATURE ONCE AGAIN ?
AND HERE GOES THE FEVER.
PINKI STUDY QUICKLY.

PINKI
DADAJI'S KURTA
STOP IT PINKI. YOU'RE TROUBLING A LOT.

OH! SOMEONE SEEMS TO HAVE COME! THE ENTIRE HOUSE IS IN A MESS.
DING-DONG...

MRS. TEENA. AFTER SO MANY DAYS? YOU SEEM TO HAVE FORGOTTEN THE WAY TODAY.
MADHU! DON'T YOU REMEMBER WE SPOKE ON THE PHONE YESTERDAY AND DECIDED TO GO FOR SHOPPING RIGHT NOW.

OH YE S ! I REMEMBER ! SINCE PINKI HAS HOLIDAYS, SHE'S BEEN CREATING A MESS IN THE HOUSE. THAT'S WHY I FORGOT.
WHY DON'T YOU SEND PINKI FOR STITCHING CLASS ?

EVEN MY DAUGHTER USED TO MAKE A LOT OF MESS . EVER SINCE SHE HAS STARTED GOING THERE SHE 'S HAPPY.

IT'S A GOOD SUGGESTION. THIS WAY PINKI WILL LEARN STITCHING.

PINKI IT'S ENOUGH. NOW QUICKLY COME FOR THE STITCHING CLASS.

I WANT TO GET PINKI ENROLLED HERE. TEACH HER HOW TO STITCH WELL.
I ASSURE YOU SHE WILL OPERATE THE STITCHING MACHINE AS SMOOTHLY AS A HORSE GALLOPS.

31

PINKI ! TAKE 2 PIECES. KEEP THEM NEXT TO EACH OTHER AND RUN THE MACHINE. THEY WILL GET JOINED.

THIS IS IT FOR TODAY. I'LL TEACH YOU MORE TOMORROW. TILL THEN PRACTICE THIS AT HOME.

WOW ! SIR TAUGHT VERY USEFUL THINGS TODAY. I'LL JOIN 2 DIFFERENT PIECES OF CLOTH AT HOME AND MOM WILL BE HAPPY.

IT SEEMS MOM HAS GONE OUT. I'LL JOIN SOME CLOTHES BEFORE SHE RETURNS. SHE'LL BE SURPRISED.

WHERE WILL I GET 2 DIFFERENT PIECES OF CLOTH FROM?

I'LL CUT THIS BED SHEET INTO 2 PARTS & THEN STITCH IT. SHE WILL BE HAPPY.

NOW I'LL JOIN BOTH THE PARTS BY STITCHING.

LOOK MOM! ON THE VERY FIRST DAY I LEARNT HOW TO JOIN 2 PIECES OF CLOTH. I WASN'T ABLE TO FIND 2 DIFFERENT PIECES SO I CUT THE BED SHEET INTO 2 PARTS AND THEN STITCHED IT.
PINKI! YOU RUINED MY NEW BED SHEET.

GET AWAY FROM MY EYES AND ALSO TAKE YOUR STITCHING MACHINE WITH YOU.

IT SEEMS I MADE A MISTAKE WHILE STITCHING WHICH ANNOYED MOM. NEXT TIME I'LL BE MORE CAREFUL.

WOW! WHAT A WONDERFUL KURTA. BUT THE TAILOR FORGOT TO STITCH ONE SLEEVE

DADAJI!
I PURCHASED THIS EXPENSIVE KURTA TO WEAR FOR TONIGHT'S PARTY. BUT THE TAILOR DIDN'T STITCH 1 SLEEVE AND I'LL HAVE TO TRAVEL 5 KMS TO GET IT STITCHED.

PINKI I'M ALREADY TROUBLED. DON'T IRRITATE ME FURTHER.
MAY BE I CAN BE OF SOME HELP.

THAT'S IT? I'LL STITCH YOUR SLEEVE JUST NOW.

REALLY ! YOU STITCH IT AND I'LL GET A COLD DRINK FOR YOU.

SIR SAID TO STITCH STRAIGHT, THEN TURN RIGHT AND THEN LEFT. NOW IT'S READY.

DADAJI ! I'VE STITCHED IT.
AND YOUR DRINK IS ALSO READY.

IT'S REALLY TASTY.
I'LL WEAR THIS AND SEE.

OH ! I'M STUCK IN THIS. HELP ME OUT FROM HERE !

PINKI
& HUNGRY KUTKUT
KUTKUT STOP! DON'T RUN HERE AND THERE. SOMETHING MIGHT BREAK.

OH! WHO'S RUINED MY SOCKS? MUST BE THIS SQUIRREL.
IT HAS RUINED MY EXPENSIVE SAREE ALSO.

MOM! KUTKUT IS HUNGRY! GIVE HER SOMETHING TO EAT.
SHUT UP! PINKI. THIS KUKU HAS MADE A BOG LOSS TO US. THROW HER OUT OF OUR HOME IMMEDIATELY

COME KUTKUT! WE'LL SEARCH FOOD FOR YOU OUTSIDE.

LOOK! HOW DO I APPEAR IN THIS GOLDEN FRAME OF YOURS?
IT SUITS YOU. YOU'RE LOOKING HANDSOME.

YOU'RE JOKING.
NO, I'M TELLING THE TRUTH. OK, NOW REMOVE IT AND PUT IT AWAY. ELSE YOU'LL HAVE A HEADACHE.

OK. I'VE KEPT IT ON THIS CHAIR SAFELY.

DADAJI, WILL KUTKUT GET SOME HELP?
PINKI! WHAT HAPPENED TO KUTKUT?
SHE'S HUNGRY SINCE MORNING. GIVE HER SOME THING TO EAT.

I HAVE SOME SNACKS WHICH I'LL GIVE TO KUTKUT.

OH !!! SHE'S CHEWED MY GOLDEN FRAME. TURN THIS SQUIRREL OUT JUST NOW.

DADAJI, AT LEAST GIVE THE SNACK TO KUTKUT.
IT DAMAGES MY THINGS AND I'LL TREAT HER ?? I DON'T WANT TO LOOK AT HER. TURN HER OUT !!

HAD YOU NOT CHEWED DADAJI'S FRAME, HE WOULD HAVE GIVEN YOU THE SNACK.

ENJOY CHILLED RASGULLAS. I'VE MADE THEM FOR YOU.
WOW RIMBI ! IT'S LOVELY ! TODAY I'LL ENJOY STOMACH FUL OF RASGULLAS.

OH GOD!!
WHAT HAPPENED?

PINKI IS COMING WITH ITS SQUIRREL.
SO WHAT?

I'LL HIDE THESE RASGULLAS. IF KUTKUT SEES THEM IT WILL EAT UP ALL OF THEM. I DON'T UNDERSTAND HOW IT MANAGES TO EAT SO MUCH.

JHAPAT JI!
PINKI TODAY YOUR AUNT AND I ARE OBSERVING A FAST. THERE'S NOTHING TO EAT. SO PLEASE GO.

YOU'RE HIDING SOMETHING FROM ME.
NOT AT ALL.

39

ARE YOU HIDING SOME EATABLE FROM ME?
OH GOD! HOW DID SHE FIND OUT? SHE MUST BE MAKING GUESSES. I'LL JUST TELL SOME INSPIRATIONAL WORDS TO HER. SHE'LL BE BORED AND WILL GO AWAY.
I DON'T HIDE ANYTHING. ALL THIS IS IN THE HANDS OF THE ONE ABOVE.

ARE YOU PLAYING HIDE AND SEEK WITH THE UNCLE LIVING UPSTAIRS? IS IT HIS TURN TO HIDE?

OH! YOU DON'T UNDERSTAND ANYTHING. I WAS TALKING ABOUT GOD. NOW YOU GO FROM HERE.

OK, I'LL LEAVE. BUT NOW YOU WON'T BE ABLE TO EAT THE THING YOU WERE HIDING FROM ME. THE CAT HAS EATEN IT.

OH! THE CAT HAS EATEN MY RASGULLAS.
MEOW!!

HAND OVER THE BAG TO ME QUIETLY AND GO AWAY.

THEN.
J-
U-
M-
P !!
TAKE THIS!! DHISHOOM!!
UNCLE! KUTKUT DOESN'T WANT A GOLD BISCUIT. SHE WANTS A REAL BISCUIT… SHE'S HUNGRY.
THAT'S IT ?? MY BISCUIT FACTORY IS NEARBY. KUTKUT CAN HAVE AS MANY BISCUITS AS SHE WANTS THERE.

THANKS PINKI. YOUR KUTKUT NOT ONLY SAVED MY LIFE BUT ALSO THIS BAG FULL OF GOLD BISCUITS FROM BEING ROBBED.
I'LL GIVE ONE BISCUIT TO HER AS A REWARD.

KUTKUT! YOUR HUNGER SHOULD BE SATISFIED NOW.

41

PINKI POLICE & THIEF

LET ME BE THE THIEF.
NO SHIRI ! YOU'LL HAVE TO BE THE POLICE.

OK.
I'LL GO AND HIDE. YOU COME TO NAB ME.

DHANNO AUNTY ! I'M THE THIEF IN THIS GAME. CAN I HIDE INSIDE YOUR HOUSE ?

RESPECTABLE PEOPLE LIVE HERE. I DON'T LET THIEVES AND ROGUES ENTER.

I'LL HIDE IN THE PARK INSTEAD.
© PRAN'S FEATURES

THAT THICK BUSH IS A PERFECT PLACE TO HIDE.

YOU !!
I'M A THIEF. HIDING HERE DUE TO THE POLICE.

ARE YOU ALSO PLAYING POLICE AND THIEF LIKE ME ?
I'M A REAL THIEF. UNDERSTAND ?

YOU'RE ALSO HIDING FROM THE POLICE LIKE ME. SO WE ARE BROTHER AND SISTER. ISN'T IT ?

OH ! DON'T PESTER ME. GO AWAY FROM HERE.

44

WHY ? IF YOU CAN HIDE IN THE BUSH, WHY CAN'T I ?
HUSH !! SPEAK SOFTLY ! IF ANYONE HEARS YOU, THE POLICE WILL FIND ME.

I'M ALSO EQUALLY AFRAID OF BEING CAUGHT LIKE YOU.

OH ! WHAT'S THIS TROUBLE ?

SPEAK SOFTLY !
YOU SPEAK SOFTLY !
YOU !
YOU !!
© PRAN'S FEATURES

QUIET ! YOU UTTER A SINGLE WORD AND I'LL KILL YOU.

45

THE LEAVES OF THAT BUSH ARE SHAKING. PINKI MUST BE HIDING THERE.

LEAVE HER! PINKI'S MY THIEF!
BEWARE! DON'T MOVE AHEAD.

DON'T YOU KNOW I'M THE POLICE?

COME.

I WAS HUNTING THIS THIEF FOR A LONG TIME NOW.
SHIRI! DO YOU KNOW HOW OPERATE A PISTOL?
WHICH PISTOL? ... THIS IS A TOY.
www.chachachaudhary.com

FIND 10 DIFFERENCES

Find the differences in two Pictures and send us back to win a surprise prize - write down the following details in block letter: Complete Name, Telephone Number with STD code (Mobile Number), Age, Place of Birth, Date of Birth, Gender, Email ID and Complete Postal Address with Pin code.

Discover Talent @ Diamond Toons

X-30, Okhla Industrial Area, Phase-II, New Delhi-110020
Ph.: 011-40712100, 40712200, E-mail: sales@dpb.in